MISSISSIPPI VISTAS

VOLUME ONE of
A MISSISSIPPI TRILOGY

Books By
LOUIS DANIEL BRODSKY

Poetry

Trilogy: A Birth Cycle (1974)
Monday's Child (1975)
The Kingdom of Gewgaw (1976)
Point of Americas II (1976)
Preparing for Incarnations (1976)
La Preciosa (1977)
Stranded in the Land of Transients (1978)
The Uncelebrated Ceremony of Pants Factory Fatso (1978)
Birds in Passage (1980)
Résumé of a Scrapegoat (1980)
Mississippi Vistas (1983) (1990)
You Can't Go Back, Exactly (1988)
The Thorough Earth (1989)
Four and Twenty Blackbirds Soaring (1989)

Bibliography (Co-authored with Robert W. Hamblin)

Selections from the William Faulkner Collection of
  Louis Daniel Brodsky: A Descriptive Catalogue (1979)

Faulkner: A Comprehensive Guide to the Brodsky Collection:
    Volume I: The Biobibliography (1982)
    Volume II: The Letters (1984)
    Volume III: The De Gaulle Story (1984)
    Volume IV: Battle Cry (1985)
    Volume V: Manuscripts and Documents (1989)

Country Lawyer and Other Stories for the Screen by
  William Faulkner (1987)

Stallion Road: A Screenplay by William Faulkner (1989)

Biography

William Faulkner, Life Glimpses (1990)

MISSISSIPPI VISTAS

VOLUME ONE of
A MISSISSIPPI TRILOGY

Poems by

Louis Daniel Brodsky

Louis Daniel Brodsky

12/28/07

St. Louis, M

TIMELESS PRESS
POETRY IN SIGHT AND SOUND
Saint Louis, Missouri

Timeless Press, Inc.
10411 Clayton Road
Saint Louis, Missouri 63131

Timeless Press books are printed on acid-free paper, and binding
materials are chosen for strength and durability.

Library of Congress Catalog Card Number: 90-70684

ISBN 1-877770-12-4
ISBN 1-877770-13-2 (pbk.)
ISBN 1-877770-14-0 (tape)
ISBN 1-877770-15-9 (tape & pbk. set)

Designed by Ruth A. Dambach
Southeast Missouri State University
Manufactured in the United States of America

First Edition, First Printing (1983)
Second Edition (Revised), First Printing (1990)

The author would like to thank the editors of the following
literary magazines for publishing and granting permission to
reprint certain poems that appear in this volume:
Kentucky Poetry Review. "The Outlander"
Parnassus Literary Journal. "The Tall Convict"
St. Andrews Review. "College Town: Friday Night"
South Carolina Review. "The Ghosts of Rowan Oak"

Lewis P. Simpson made suggestions that strengthened the
structure of the original manuscript Malcolm Cowley edited for the
1983 First Edition of *Mississippi Vistas*, published for the
University of Mississippi Center for the Study of Southern Culture
by University Press of Mississippi. That edition sold out 1500
hardback copies by 1985.

This completely revised and reset Second Edition has benefited
from careful readings by Bruce Alan Grossman. Jane Goldberg,
Managing Editor of Timeless Press, deserves singular
commendation for her relentless quest for the "perfect text."

For
Cleanth Brooks
Malcolm Cowley
Lewis P. Simpson
and
Robert Penn Warren

These distinguished men of American Letters
have personally given me
a generous measure of their sensitive intelligence;
to them I am indebted beyond all my measures.

If there be grief, let it be the rain
And this but silver grief, for grieving's sake,
And these green woods be dreaming here to wake
Within my heart, if I should rouse again.

But I shall sleep, for where is any death
While in these blue hills slumbrous overhead
I'm rooted like a tree? Though I be dead
This soil that holds me fast will find me breath.

"My Epitaph" — William Faulkner

Contents

TOWNSPEOPLE

ROWAN OAK AND THE GHOSTS OF YOKNAPATAWPHA

MISSISSIPPI VISTAS

VOLUME ONE of
A MISSISSIPPI TRILOGY

THE OUTLANDER

As the Crow Flies

There are no crows flying today;
Only my loneliness
Rides south toward a destination
Intuition alone knows.

As I go, whiteness disintegrates
As though yesterday's blizzard
Were a cosmic joke
Devised by a necromancer

Instead of high- and low-pressure zones
Blown over November's shoulders
By converging fates;
A joke without a punch line,

Unless, of course,
One considers black humor appropriate
And interprets the snow,
A natural phenomenon,

As God's class action suit
Against this state
For perpetuating discrimination
And racial unrest.

Up ahead, the entire gray horizon
Is streaked with saffron shafts,
A fusillade aimed at me,
Illuminating the design of my flight:

I'm a Northern apologist,
Scion of the original Tribe of Oppression,
An abolitionist preaching civil rights,
Jim Crow poet

Traveling straight as an arrow
Toward a podium located at Ole Miss
From which I'll protest
Snow, loneliness, and necromantic jokers.

An Accompaniment to the Rain

All the way down past Cape,
Sikeston, New Madrid, and Hayti
To Blytheville, through Memphis
And on into Oxford off I-55,
The rain reiterated its slow, silver grief
As though someone in the celestial order
Had suffered a reversal of fate.

By the time I arrived six hours later,
The sky had cried itself out;
Streets were dry, and lush growth,
Imperceptibly dripping,
Was already sapping July's humidity.
Indeed, by evening, I'd even forgotten
The funeral that had taken place

In which I, at the head of a cortège,
Had led the procession of one,
Transporting a spirit from its sweet retreat
Among family and friends,
Into a land of strange, vacant faces.
In fact, I'd not even recognized myself
As the dead man lying in state.

Even now, surrounded by white silence,
Rowan Oak's solitude disguises the nature
Of my transfiguration. Strolling slowly
Into the fragrance of Bailey's Woods,
I wade deeper, as into an ocean,
Knowing only my ghost will return home
To my wife, my children, myself.

Trying to Conceive

As I veer east at Greenville
And commence the desolate trek across the Delta,
Innumerable looming clouds
Force themselves on my senses
Like condescending thoughts; at once
They put my intellect on the defensive.

Images within my kindled cauldron
Scuffle over which will gain freedom,
Whose metaphor will achieve preeminence,
Be chosen for originality and relevance.
They fight like a thousand minnows
Reaching for the same breadcrumb.

By the time the fittest vision
Rises to the mind's surface
To be pedestaled, festooned, and admired
By the poet who stirs behind my eyes,
The sky, a fully dilated kaleidoscope,
Is totally erased; it requires refocusing.

Once more the cauldron roars with metaphors
Giddy and extravagant as adolescents
Just discovering their sexuality.
As a fresh description slips over the edge,
Rain cancels its appropriateness;
Again the brain must consider its options.

But now its fires are too cool
To regenerate my poetic sensibilities.
Painfully I watch the Delta,
Devoured by kudzu, dissolve into rain
As I transport my aborted brainseeds
Toward the City of the Inane.

Spectator

Traversing the verdant Delta
From West Helena, Arkansas, to Greenville,
Mississippi, I'm spelled by Old Man's aura;
My eyes sieve the humidity
To retrieve meaning from the land's design:

Combines winding amber harvest
Out of fields onto spools
Revolving before them;
Lackadaisical blacks with hoes
Weeding in the ferocious heat;

Tractors, maneuvering through young cotton,
Spraying for owners
Too poor to afford dusters;
Crops flowing down the season
That nourishes this region

And justifies its existence,
Whose economy owes its survival,
Not so much to feudal ways
As to natural faith and Acts of God;
This Nile-like civilization,

Desecrated by a few
Who, conceiving in tenancy
A means to riches and security
While denying multitudes personal liberty,
Would squeeze penury dry.

Driving south,
I'm staggered by the abundance of poverty:
Ramshackle cabins
Outnumbering prefabricated "planations"
Ten thousand to one;

Defunct country stores, gas stations,
Public schools run by mice,
Snakes, and birds nesting inside;
Derelict cars and oxidizing biplanes
Huddling beside trailers like cataleptic buzzards;

And, ultimately, the diabolical sun
Proclaiming defeat of the enemy, Man,
In this doomed basin
Where relief is unobtainable, except for me,
A free agent retaining my insularity.

I'm old Ike McCaslin,
Recapitulating truths in commissary ledgers
I write and recite to myself,
Repudiating the futility of poetic rhetoric
To imbue life with vital solutions.

Oxford

Oxford is another night away from home.
In The Warehouse, my wiry hair,
A thorn-crown silhouetted by overhead lights,
Snares in words on my wine-smeared page.

Here, my blank heart's bleary stare
Shares the smoky, opaque air
With fifty pairs of groping eyes,
Trying to achieve transcendency

In the cold brain's hot rain
By writing intoxicated poetry.
Oxford is Youth's green-lit dock
Flashing erratically in middle age.

But doomed to disillusioned dreams
And unreciprocated faith
In creativity's redemptive mystique,
I keep hearing Faulknerian echoes in the gloom.

Oxford is Circe, Scylla, Lorelei
Luring me toward her
To suffer the horror of dying unborn
Within whispers of a living aura.

A Guest Lecturer Rehearses

Far from home
In this nameless Oxford bar
Where college jocks swill beer by the schooner,
And Temple Drakes, at bargain rates,
Twirl verbal batons
And smoke "gold" dope for a lark,
I'm a victim of clock-block, place-stasis,
A monument to nonmomentum;
Ozymandias with his shattered visage
Scattered among the sands;
An unoxygenated fire gasping for breath;
A baby contracting back into the womb.

Where and When
Descend the mind's stairs to its basement
And are placed in storage bags
By the Keeper of Obsolete Adverbs;
Fastidiously She labels each piece
Of my dismantled sensibility
Before sealing the crypt
In which She'll keep me waiting
For a writ of habeas corpus, indeterminately.
Meanwhile, chilled Chablis
Unwinds my taut-wound springs;
My numb skeleton dissolves into the din

While its flesh remains inflated
Over inebriated arteries and veins.
Suddenly the music stops:
Such abrupt lack of distraction
Cracks my wine glass, whose flood
Has drowned out ratiocination.
As its last drop drips to my lips,
I feel my body flowing back to my touch
And hear a distant voice echoing
As if from the depths of an artesian well,
Beckoning me to begin my lecture:
Slurring my words, I address the empty room.

Held Fast to the Past

Although I've driven automatically
For at least two hours,
A persistence of imagery
Has kept memory's transmission
Locked in neutral. Kudzu,
Long changed from lascivious green
To ineffectual coils
Hanging in midair, nowhere attached,
Like Piranesian carceri chains,
Still fills the tangled space
Between windshield and imagination
My dull eyes try feverishly to penetrate;
Hissing like spitting cobras,
These plants blind me to the road ahead.

Whether these reptilian visions
Derive from innate pusillanimity,
Superstitiousness, or poor circulation
From sitting in one position
Too long, I can't say.
Definitely they've infected my brain.
I hear lubricious slithering
Just above my eyes
As though they might be nesting
In my spongy hemispheres
Or consuming themselves in crazed mating.
Possibly these tenacious vines
Intend to render me supine
Before I arrive home.

Now the highway begins to sway
Like a rope bridge in a rude wind.
Hallucinations overtake my vehicle,
Enveloping fear in density
So stifling,
Suffocation might be more desirable.
Skidding to a halt on the shoulder,
I wait for the tremor to abate
And try to fathom why
That damned plant has been stalking me,
Literally, through my eyes,
Gnawing on my thoughts.
Suddenly I know its tropism;
It's my fecund imagination the kudzu craves.

Writer in Flight

This gloomy, humid morning
Is another doomed Mississippi a.m.
Through which my startled spirit slips
Like wind past weather stripping,
Confusing vision with spectral images
Of Percy Grimm, the ancient Snake,
And a dispossessed pariah, Isaac McCaslin.

Why I'm constantly haunted and cursed
By such chimeras baffles me.
Yet these insidious demons
Persist in pitting my stomach with abrasions,
Spitting acidic epithets in my face,
Castrating my hopes for a safe passage
As I travel north toward home.

Up I-55, Memphis looms,
A huge, human amoeba endlessly extending.
I can't avoid its suffocating grasp
No matter how tenuous
My connection; its arteries
Sluice me through to the extremities
Of its slimy skin. Suddenly I cringe,

Pray I'll reach the River and escape
To the contiguous land of relative solemnity.
Cypress bayous and pines
Disappear into my rearview mirror;
The Great State of Tennessee materializes,
New Jerusalem welcomes me.
Soon Missouri will reclaim its Wandering Jew.

For now, Arkansas and two hundred miles
Separate my fate from the greater Fate
Ordaining the rotation of bodies
Terrestrial and ethereal; I sigh,
Realizing Time has hung me from its fob,
Suspended my four-wheeled chrysalis
In a perfectly regulated orbit

About the unknown sum of years
I'll maneuver through completing my trip.
I drive on, no longer daunted
By chimeras, grotesques, or psychic parasites.
Once more, my ego has gained suzerainty,
Freed me to write apostrophes to Life —
Arriving is forever just up ahead.

Kudzu

Bilious and livid tongues of kudzu,
Clumped lasciviously over the road's lips,
Wag in the back-blown wash
Of passing cars like dissolute hitchhikers
Thumbing drunkenly to Oblivion
Or slobbering hunchbacks
Ready to jump into my path.

I succumb to their jeers
And witness their seething green appearance,
Encroaching on the nervous wilderness,
Change to tattered wrappings
Smothering tree-mummies
Embalmed in Mississippi's brittle immolation.
A photosynthetic putrescence lingers;

Dionysian gloom chews the hills,
Gluts its tumescent gut
On untainted Nature
Without leaving room to dispose of its waste.
Suddenly the kudzu metamorphoses
Into a million, moiling, hooded cobras
Coiling to strike me before I reach home.

The Tall Convict

On my trip home up I-55
I cross the Tallahatchie River,
Running swiftly under the highway,
And watch it disappear in my rearview mirror
Like a silver sliver slithering skyward
Through a Flemish landscape painting,
Meandering into silent space.

Again gazing ahead,
I sense myself afloat on this road
Banked by pine trees three rows deep,
Almost as if the river's perpendicularity
Has merged with this concrete Old Man
And is now flowing vertically
Toward its own focal point on the horizon.

Fleeing Mississippi this murky morning,
I feel my eyes submit to its current.
A convict trying to slip the bonds
Of fluid uprootedness and keep from drowning
In too much freedom,
I worry whether I'll be carried upstream
Or deposited down here, permanently.

The Outlander

All the way past Batesville
From Oxford, loblolly giants follow me.
Visions of their shingle-barked trunks,
Glimpsed peripherally,
Contrast the sky's dark blue interstices.
Distant voices, lifting from Mississippi's hills,
Remind me of troops, ragged regiments,
That irretrievably doomed Gray army
Of old men conscripted like duteous youth.

Fantasies riddle my mind's hide
Like double loads of grapeshot
Wadded in invisible, smokeless charges;
The trees seem to be retreating behind me.
Involuntarily I've become their leader
Mounted on a foundered nag, guiding them home
From that urn-like moment at Gettysburg
Prior to Pickett's blind rush
From an old order, as if to reverse Time.

But the turning point had been reached
So long ago, defeat signed
Into treaty, acquiesced to reluctantly,
If never really assimilated in deed,
That I can't fathom their hushed design
This early April morning,
Their need to attach, like wombseeds,
To my imagination's placental ceiling.
Perhaps they've mistaken me for their messiah;

Possibly they've confused my vehicle
With a bullet shuttle that might pick them up
As threads, zoom through a loom,
And weave them into a fine, new uniform
To be worn at a presidential inauguration.
Whatever the occasion, their shadowy weight
Has made my passage oppressive.
Maybe, by detaining my spirit, these pines
Hope to gain a final shot at the Enemy.

THE LAND
AND ITS INHABITANTS

Hanging Out the Wash

Although I pass in seconds,
My fleet eyes see her entire life
Arrested in that singularly echoing gesture:
Her fat, black body,
Clad in peach tatters, stretching forever
Against a full-throated wind,
Trying mightily to pin a dingy white sheet
To a line and keep it from blowing
Out of her grip, with her tangled in it,

Fearing, perhaps, her own disappearance,
Possibly cursing under her breath
The additional insult to her burdensome work,
But most likely, slightly sighing
Before summoning from unthinking
Just enough energy
To gyve it, retrieve other wet pieces,
And let them dry before sunset.
I can almost smell the freshness of her poverty.

Signs of the Times

For Faye Wallace and Nancy Cooper

No diesel fuel. Too much rain.
Jesus, the fields are still unplowed,
Fallow as Vestal Virgins.
Leaking drums, corroded from pesticides,
Dissolve runways
Beneath idle biplanes.
Even massive tractors,
Frustrated and impatient, remain static;
Their folded disc gangs,
Clinging slavishly to their backs
Just above power takeoffs,
Are wings of buzzards
Poised to shred the earth's dead flesh.
May submits without complaint.

Nowhere in this rain-plagued cradle
Are there signs of living inhabitants;
Even snakes have fled inundated brakes.
Where, last year, stands of cotton
Crowded tenants off the land,
Pernicious weeds, impervious to flooding,
Fill old furrows like hobos in curbs.
Up in Memphis, down in New Orleans,
Nervous bankers, brokers,
And restless investors twiddle their thumbs,
Play poker over beers and martinis,
While near Helena, Tunica, and Hughes,
Blacks and whites commune in fear
As their livelihood disappears without a fight.

Delta Porch People

No one particular time of day
Can be isolated positively from the rest
To suggest heat has reached apogee.
Afternoon bubbles in morning's cauldron,
Dusk is poured slowly into night's mold;
Delta furnace fires are never banked.

Breathing reeks of the leper's flesh;
Lethargy stalls,
Crawls from curb to shack and back,
Waiting for blacks to "catch up";
Wizened patriarchs and obese Dilseys
Dominate pigtailed, barefooted shades

Who play mumbledypeg all day long
With truant dust motes.
Their dull hopes are knives thrown
And empty dreams broken blades
That won't take hold
In parched yards where they grow old.

Days fade into generations each evening
As cicadas' leggy monotones
Unloose turgid air into thermal eddies
Miragelike, trivial, toward unnecessary stars.
The old people in rocking chairs on porches
Watch for Autumn's moondog

While their impatient offspring
Go crazy from adolescent spider bites,
Come home groping on hands and knees,
Begging for a place to sleep.
Even their undreamed babies
Know the omen of creaking floor boards.

Pecan Grove

Driving through this drought-plagued cradle,
Past illimitable fields
Of unbolled, flowerless cotton,
Inactive gins,
Yellow-leafed soybeans,
And idle, radial-engined, bi-wing dusters,

I notice an isolated pecan grove
Off to one side.
Amidst all this bright, inexorable dying,
Ordained by unpropitiable gods,
It rises like a Renaissance cathedral
Shimmering on a French plain.

Its shaded clearing,
A velvet robe draped at royalty's feet,
Invites me, with curious inarticulateness,
To come inside, repair from the glare,
And luxuriate in Delta sleep
Before resuming my chase after elusive miles.

Seeing the ceiling of Above from underneath
Is like looking through the eyes of a dove
Flying upside down
Or glancing over a raindrop's shoulder
On its journey earthward;
I'm a baby groping for its mother's teat.

Never have I dreamed
That a mere clearing in Mississippi,
Filled with such lush clusters,
Could be a cool-breathing cave,
A heated deep-sea grot, house of worship,
Or reachable mirage.

Yet resting in this anomalous place,
Lulled into mystical distillations
By vehicles slipping past
Sporadically,
I awaken to the kinship
Between oasis and blistering desert.

All at once my senses fathom
That the truest, quickest distance
Connecting incongruities in the figmental mind
Is the time it takes to recognize
Divine design
In both — death and life.

Slaves

Still they're slaves — all of them,
White and black alike;
Slaves to the fields, potential mildew,
Rust, blight, and "beneficial bugs"
Too early exposed to insecticides
Upsetting Nature's metabolism;
Slaves to rainfall, "harmfuls,"
Their own paranoias,
And ghosts of ancient plantation owners;
Slaves to vagaries of being shipped back,
Black and white alike,
The one "race" to Africa's Gambia,
The other, those rascally scions of Byrd
And Oglethorpe, to the "Old Bailey"
Once crops fail to mature,
Futures bankrupt guarantors,
Notes come due on loans,
And machinery is coldly repossessed.

Slaves subordinated to King Cotton
Swelter in their vassalage;
And all classes live under one Rule,
Whether retiring at day's edge
To ramshackle cabin
Or lordly manor house
Bordered on all sides by plants
Growing right up to their doorsteps.
These human beings,
Indistinguishable in their primate pacings,
Are sleeping souls
Dreaming dreams they keep awake each season
Of one day being shed
Not only of delicate crops,
But also each other,
Black hand, white landowner alike.

One more time, anyway,
Compresses, combines, tractors, and gins
Begin to whine; their reiterations
Fill the air with the ancient call
Almost every inhabitant of the Midsouth
Has responded to all his life,
Despite laziness, insurmountable biases,
Physical pain, and psychic abomination.
A sibilant excitement is abroad.
Soon the land will exact its tithes
In sweat, fatigue, and anxiety
From "cain see" to "caint see."
And each family will submit its allegiance,
As always, to communal duties
Done in the name of an obsolete monarchy.

Time's Harvest

Whining combines, grinding in tandem,
Pillage the fields,
Wrest their precious golden pleasures
Before setting dust adrift,
Leaving in their wake stubble specters,
Vaporous surrogates,
Crones, and moaning widows
Praying for November winds
To redeem them from barrenness and old age
By assimilating their stray seeds:
The Land recoils in shame from its desuetude.

Now across the broad Delta, and as deep,
A ubiquitous conflagration
Of smouldering, black shrouds
Rises above flames
Articulating shrill crying voices.
Soon no trace of harvest
Will mar the terrain;
Shoots and blooms will burst from silence
Like maidens in petticoats, silk hose,
And lacy pinafores dancing the Maypole,
Their hands braiding the sun's slanting rays.

Shall Inherit

For Evans Harrington
and Ann Abadie

Traversing easterly from West Helena,
The primordial Delta
Awakens me to my own impoverishment
By exposing my eyes
To black tenant shacks
Squatting like disreputable buzzards;
Sheets drying on lines
Are their breeze-ruffled feathers
That distract and take my gaze
In one fell swoop
From daydreaming to actual poverty.

If I were forced to speculate,
Chance and Circumstance
Would be mythical sisters
In my doomsayer's conclusion
That Fate has cursed this land
And its people irreversibly.
But my guts
Reject such literary formulation,
Demand more compelling metaphors
To foretell the Delta's future
And dispel its past.

Suddenly I'm plowing these fields
On a mulish tractor,
Eating collard greens, turnips, hominy,
Groping on all fours picking cotton bolls;
Dust clogs my nostrils,
Flood-mud oozes through my toes
While that damned sun
Indelibly tans my skin to a crisp.
Disfranchised, as at birth,
I'm born to the nature of divinity:
God's chosen hover close to the earth.

Drought in the Midsouth

Waiting inexorably
For the slightest sign of rain,
They awaken each hazy, humid dawn
Making oblations to Demeter,
And beg superstitious beliefs
To bring them brief relief.

Exasperated, they take naps
To ward off depression;
They've learned that even prayer
Can't inflate stunted stalks
Of runt-sized cotton
Or straighten drooping beans.

Food tastes like soil
Fertilized with ammonia and pesticides.
Grace, humbly mumbled,
Can't be distinguished from slurs
Cursing the plague-infecting Enemy.
Friend and neighbor alike

Know to the precise hour and second
Just how long
The interim between July 4th
And this late-August moment has been
Since rain last broke
Its dry silence and spoke to them.

During this season,
The sky's only moisture
Has been that of artificial chemicals
Cascading at great cost
From bi-wing planes
Flown by pilots hired to spray.

Even sleep is a prolongation
Of consternation
And fear that the very next hour
Their crops will be doomed,
Property foreclosed,
Patrician names shamed and forgotten.

Yet they continue to watch closely
The process by which cotton and beans
Grow slowly moribund
In a land of rainless tributaries
Where planters are inundated
By their own silent weeping.

Gone Fishing

For miles, the highway I drive
Rolls out like a dream attenuating
Or gay-colored thread
Being spun by a weaving machine,
Then stitched into garments
Neatly fitted to my carefree heart.
I wear this morning comfortably.

Suddenly I rush past a black man
Shouldering bamboo poles,
His wife, straggling behind,
Carrying a newborn wrapped in burlap,
With five barefooted children
Following like baby ducks,
All imperturbably navigating road's edge.

Our gam shatters my daydreaming,
Thrusts me back to fact
And relocates me in major desolation.
Those corn-rowed pickaninnies
And nappy-headed boys in torn corduroys
Project my tight-throated focus
Onto my own children, home in school.

But as I hasten toward Oxford
To avoid missing business,
Losing commissions vital to my position,
Those eight souls
Reverse their hold over my pity.
They'll catch freedom's limit today;
I'll not get a bite!

Elegy South

This mid-November, I bear witness
To the Delta's embalmment;
Almost nothing remains
Of scraggly-tufted cotton plants
Recently plowed under
Except puffs missed by picker and disc.
Grain dust and stubble
Smoulder in neighboring fields;
Even wilted soybeans
Withdraw beneath turned earth
As planters prepare to reanoint it
With quick-rooting winter wheat seeds.

Emptiness pervades this land
Whether it's sleeping between seasons
Or briefly resting, catching its breath
Before accepting the next crop.
Nevertheless, these fields
Have achieved majestic quiescence
In submitting to death.
Their surrender is Eternity at work
Engendering wider circles,
Deeper furrows — continuity.
Today I seed the earth with my words
And pray for tomorrow's harvest.

A Delta Planter Returns Home

In air astir with dragonflies,
Pines melt into Delta cotton.
Batesville, Marks,
And Clarksdale arrive and recede
As I drive toward Old Man
Lying torpidly as a glutted snake
Sunning on a log.

Ever westerly,
I go past dogtrot hovels
Whose parked tractors and plows
Are like obsolete parts
Cluttering hardware store shelves.

Compresses and gins
Seem impatient in their silence
During this hiatus
Through which crop dusters fly,
Maneuvering under telephone lines,
Nearly shearing low hedgerows
As they knot and unknot the sky's bow ties.

Suddenly these images are obliterated
By invisible, viscid spray
Raining into my brain like insecticides —
Paranoias and hallucinations
Mississippi engenders in me naturally.

The levee alongside, to my left,
Breaks wide open;
I'm inundated by its rapid collapse,
Washed away like topsoil,
And scattered farther and farther
Until I no longer recognize the location
Where motion deposits me.

But curiously, my flesh seems cleansed,
My mind free to plant its seeds.
I sense myself being absorbed,
Rooting, growing toward home
As one season yields to the next.

TOWNSPEOPLE

Chiaroscuro

We've made such academic fuss
Over the Land, its People, and their Past
As fundamental pedagogical criteria
For understanding William Faulkner's fiction,

That, as I sit beside a black man in bibs,
Breathing his gentle stench
In the humid, bench-strewn shadows
Beneath Oxford's squatty Courthouse,

Catching glimpses of the dogtrot dreams
He shades from the blazing sun
Behind glassy, leonine eyes and balances
On the tip of his tight-lipped conditioning,

I chastise myself for having forgotten
How elemental people really are,
And just how consummately incidental
The skillfully ingenious criticism seems

To the writer, too obsessed by creation
To ponder the implications of his symbols,
And for the Ethiope, who, having inherited
The family crest, refuses to question his flesh.

As keepers of our fathers' wisdom, we two,
Unknown "Jew poet" and "useless nigger,"
Acquit each other of prejudice
And subterfuge with our silent, speaking smiles.

Addie's Agony

6:25 a.m.
Is just another undisclosing shape
In morning's attenuated mosaic of hours
Waving me off.
My escape is neither ritual
Nor sacrament,
But rather a sanctimonious act,
Empty of all meaning,
Abstracted to incomprehensibility.

This green, steamy countryside
Named Ste. Genevieve,
Into whose misty oblivion I slip,
Gives its gifts as unselfconsciously
As the Savior nearing Golgotha
Miming supplications;
It provides insight into the solemnity
And happiness of brainless things,
Reinforces my need for peace.

Cows lolling in stolid muteness
Moo so loudly
Through this fertile desolation,
I fear my slightest miscue
Could make them stampede my cortège.
Spring-fed ponds and creeks,
Whose undisturbed surfaces
Are Nature's hymens,
Refuse to reflect my vagrant design.

I'm dying to enter the earth alive,
Dive into my stream of consciousness,
Penetrate Poesy, and emerge,
Purged of my dependence on words,
Able to fashion Truth from absolute silence.
Even the waxy trees,
Looming in stately profusion,
Remind me how puny I am,
How human my destiny.

Now a vague putrescence
Permeates this vessel that's coffined me
In these word-cursed years,
Going from one exit to the next.
Perhaps on this final excursion,
Anse will respect my wishes
To be transported to the source
Where dying is just a matter of getting ready
To stay alive forever.

Gowan's Enchantment

Yesterday afternoon,
Just as a reluctant southern sun
Funneled into blue pine hills beyond Oxford,
I was unexpectedly spelled
By a shimmering semblance of Temple Drake,
The governor's golden co-ed.

She entered my eyes,
Penetrated my senses like wine,
Entranced the sentries standing guard
Outside my somnolent conscience,
And danced naked on the stage
My dreams had erected for sublimated lovers.

Momentarily, from a distance of years,
As I leered at her without speaking,
A convergence of our lusty spirits,
Whispering furtively, occurred;
Then lights, music, and voices,
Amplified by inebriation, destroyed the philter

Connecting us with shadows
Cast by a spider crosshatching sunrays.
Briefly we'd meshed, released seeds, unclung;
Then suddenly she'd run from my fantasy
Into the arms of a barfly
With whom she'd get drunk and later fuck.

Eternal Triangle

Lilac, oleander, and crape myrtle
Decorate this lost day
Disappearing through a magnolia-hued twilight
Into an antebellum evening
Draped with wisteria and honeysuckle vines;
Their sweet, lingering scents
Mingle with whiskey sours
That transport my mind
Toward a timeless, watery vortex.

Through a carnival glass snifter
I witness Quentin dissolve
Down murky fathoms of the Charles River,
Weighted with six-pound flatirons
Tied to ideas of pride
Conceived in shame —
Obsessive, incestuous, and obsolete.
His drowning confounds me.
The pain of his violent suicide

Knells inside tiny, gurgling bubbles
Ballooning to my ears' surfaces
Like off-key carillon bells
Transposing old dirges to cacophonies.
As they rise higher,
Their overtones diminish to kisses
Dripping from his wizened lips
Reaching to touch his sister
Before she races from his bursting veins.

She withstands the pressure.
But his empty confession,
Conceived to vindicate her unblessed soul,
Is swallowed whole by a trout
Skimming for flies in a nearby stream.
Now only I exist
To interpret the persistent echo
Of the feisty little girl in muddy drawers
Begging me to take her home.

Dilsey

This day dawns bleak and chill
Like Dilsey's vision of the Compson decay,

And as I traverse my stark hallucinations,
Searching for the proper exit
To escape their hold over me,
I see in the shadowy, swirling sky
Her apocalyptic specters
Bearing down on my progress from above.

A gray gloom fills the rooms
Through which Benjy
Drags his empty spermbag,
Trying to decide which way
To turn the key that unlocks words
Doomed to cells of slobber and moaning.

Even the humid silence
Absorbs echoes of long-ago nights
When Youth climbed down the drainpipe
To rendezvous with its own supple odor
And found, instead, lust waiting
To ferry it forever from its safe abode.

This day is Quentin masturbating;
Caddy come home,
Crying on spying her motherless child;
Jason ranting outside his hardware store,
Cursing lightning and thunder of a migraine storm;
And father drowning in his inebriated rhetoric.

Suddenly my windshield is splattered
With silver blood; she's grieving for me, too.

Miss Emily

The soul's topiary grows monstrous
With neglect. No one
Seems to live on the grounds anymore
Or come at orderly intervals
To trim, mow, and hoe formal gardens
Infested with weeds and mimosa seedlings
Sprouting in grostesque profusion
From its ghostly, eroded beds.

It's been at least ten years
Since we townspeople perceived lights
Lambent at night
In the old mansion's eccentric eyes
Or noticed comings and goings
Of Homers paying social visits,
Making service calls, collecting taxes;
Ten years since lightning struck,

Ripping through the attic,
Collapsing the chimney inwards
Brick by brick, and setting fire to rooms
In which peacefully sleeping fantasies reposed,
Extinguishing evanescently
The fragile, passionate desires
Of one who yet hides
In the charred depths of her antique edifice.

Actually, even now,
Despite surviving an anorexic spirit,
She's still too mortified to come outside,
Submit her memories to fresh air,
And witness them disintegrate.
It's been ten years, or more,
Since we last glimpsed her naked soul
Cavorting in the gardens under magnolia-rain.

Summer Afternoon Idyll

For Joan Williams

Muscadine grows lengthwise
And skyward;
Its juicy, tumescent redolence,
A godly suspension
Entwined with ripe scuppernong clusters
Vining along the clapboard siding,
Festoons my drowsy eyes,
Suffocates me
In languorous scents of Mississippi.

I, a virgin easily surfeited,
Desiring sweet inebriation
And the reeling feeling
Of escaping the seasons
By violating hymeneal daydreams
With psychic semen,
Submit to its aromatic aphrodisiac.
But my dreamseeds
Fertilize only the fallen grapes.

College Town: Friday Night

As I sit on this enclosed patio
Of Oxford's most animated watering hole,
I'm assailed by an agonizing desire
To know who in Hell
Invented higher learning —
The pursuit of degrees, tenure, celebrity
Through publication of treatises,
Tracts, novels, and poetry —
And just how this cottage industry,
This self-perpetuating phenomenon,
Ever got started
From such modest, innocuous beginnings.

Uninitiates to this historic moment
Might never guess
That these children, dressed in frivolity
And timeless irresponsibility,
Are descendants of scions begot of lovers
Copulating beyond latitudes
Bordering the blessed Hesperides.
A totemistic freedom persists here:
They tip their wine glasses to the winds
And sip as if Oblivion
Would irresistibly drip to their lips,
Then whisper to low-flying Artemis,

Hoping to persuade her handmaidens
To abet their basest venalities,
Grant their wishes to fuck
God's own personal mistress.
She regards such gross obscenities
As adolescent indiscretions,
Crude, futile, ludicrous attempts
At emulating the lotus-eaters,
Progenitors of their vile tribe.
Meanwhile, the clitoral music
Begins to stroke their blown minds
To heights of inebriated nightglitter;

Obsessed with cosmic fornication,
They become goats and "slithy toads"
Roaming with desperate lasciviousness
In quest of lesbian queens
And glass-slippered princesses
Writhing in sweaty sleep
Between sheets wet from semenseeds
Conceived by priapic incubi.
Finally, shepherded by fleecy dreams
Beyond nightmare's reach,
They climb mountains of volcanic desire
And are buried alive under human magma.

Curiously, I no longer feel alienated
From these wastrel souls
Converging on this place where spirits,
Ceaselessly flowing from fountains
Spewing Chablis and rosé,
Tinge the air with voluptuousness
Redolent of lovemaking.
I speak to passing ladies
And their lassitudinous swains;
We reassure ourselves that happiness
And being honest with each other's feelings
Are absolutely "where it's at."

At their request, I quote poems
Scrawled on cave walls behind their eyes
As though I were a circus vendor
Blowing up odes
And let them billow into the sky
Like beautiful helium balloons.
My whisperous recitations
Subvert their flirtatiousness
To overt concupiscence;
They listen while I scribble elegies
Across their sensual cells, down their spines
In the gentlest measured graffiti.

Enchanted, we rhyme ourselves into a circle,
Who've been total strangers
Until this moment
When touching dismantles the drywall
Separating well-insulated rooms
We've leased from a common landlord.
We enter each other for the first time.
Suddenly I know who in Hell
Invented higher learning and why —
God bequeathed us this retreat
In which to revel sexually and luxuriate
Before dying into life, eternally.

Quentin at Ole Miss

Each morning for a week,
I've awakened at twilight
To the cosmic sounds of education
Being constructed from the ground up:

Air compressors whining like hyenas,
Objects dropping from heights,
Hard-hatted blacks and whites
In T-shirts, shouting cryptically,

Hacking away at emptiness
To complete the concrete Tinkertoy
Here at Ole Miss
Before the start of classes.

A crane takes my gaze
In every direction it moves,
Swaying like a dangling spider
Threatening me with malignity.

My mind eludes its slow halo,
Emerges, like Noah,
From its dark ark
Into August's pulverized luminosity.

Yet something's changed today;
An unearthly quietude pervades this place,
Silences me inside a Sunday sleep
My eyes and ears can't differentiate

From deathly numbness.
My stupefaction blackens the sun.
I lack insight and initiative
To grope for my stymied soul's exact location.

Whether I'm at the precipice
Of an old epoch or new abyss,
Poised to soar or plunge,
Remains for the next few moments to disclose.

Meanwhile I listen for oracles
That might confirm life exists on this campus
Where my solitary, unendowed intellect
Has spent its best years hiding.

Suddenly my mind identifies this silence
As the kiss God gives His ministers
Before He sends them
Into the heart's still wilderness to die.

Oxford Nocturne

Last evening we sat outside
Admiring the giant, talismanic moon,
Listening to soft-struck overtones
From the cupolaed Courthouse
Dissipating in the humid gloom of midnight,
Then one, then two.

And we talked of Aristotle's *Poetics*,
Faulkner's epicene women,
His early fascination with nympholepsy,
Hermaphroditism, and romantic chastity,
Nixon's blatant abrogation of truth,
Kennedy's mistresses, and Tinker Bell.

She dreamed aloud her drowsy wishes
To stay awake forever,
Crowd her life with gentle lovers,
And be crowned Queen
Of New Orleans society, "called out"
To dance with every masked Cyrano.

He incorporated in the chain she wove
Gold links of his own fancy,
Pretending to be her redeemer, Lothario,
Capable of satisfying her insatiable desires,
Making her serve his effeminate ends
By mastering her writhing psyche.

I reeled and teetered vertiginously
On my earthly highwire,
Balancing them both with poetical skepticism,
Twice missed my footing
And nearly plunged into the netless abyss
Defining the desolation of our desperate lives.

Now morning is a cranial throb;
The sun's rubbish pile
Burns in the middle of a landfill
Whose gaseous effluvium suffocates bell notes
Choking in the throat of the Courthouse.
Our talk is of coffee, aspirin; Faulkner is dead.

We've resumed our doomed pretenses,
Assumed Ku Klux suit and tie,
Respectable, ethical deferences —
Resigned to teach school, prepare briefs,
Versify, and forget how our delusions
Almost freed us from the rest of our lives.

Reverend Whitfield's Apostasy

Last fall,
I lay on my back
On a quilt Nature had stitched
From brittle leaves of the ancient Osage orange
That bordered Bailey's Woods.
Gazing up at its black, barky branches
Redolent of tarantula legs,
I was transfixed, not in fear,
But rather amazed that my relaxed apparatus
Might isolate and extract from abstraction
Such an ominously concrete image-cluster
To fluster my moment's repose.

Yet the longer I stared
The sharper grew my hallucination:
I wasn't a votary come in humbleness,
But an interloper at Rowan Oak
The tree had caught in its web,
A witness to its pendular descent
As it poised to bite, paralyze,
And consume my apostate conscience in its juices.

Today, curiosity has remembered me
To this spot where I'd died. Lying on my back
Beneath the green, blooming Osage orange,
No stone nor stick recogizes me
Though it was here, once, I'd come alone
To dream and pray that Addie
Would sneak from the Woods and consummate desire;
Here I'd anxiously returned last fall,
Hoping to repeat the bejeweling of our deeds
Before fleeing to my family,
Retreating to my heart's empty temple
Without waiting to see if she would reappear.

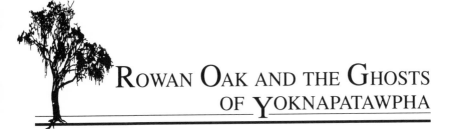

ROWAN OAK AND THE GHOSTS OF YOKNAPATAWPHA

The Ghosts of Rowan Oak

For Eva Miller

The kept lawn is alive with ants
Marching single file
Over a million Roman roads,
Traversing a thousand grassy aqueducts,
Besieging myriad Thermopylaes
To reach the citadel of my seated being.

Cedars, inspired by Old Ionic breezes,
Acknowledge these presences below,
Sing a Greek chorus for Agamemnon
And stranded Odysseus only I can hear
For their roistering at Rowan Oak.
A voice is weeping in the nearby Woods;

Perhaps shadows are practicing elocution,
Or the temple's pillared portico
Is creaking under the weight of my gaze;
Possibly Faulkner's ghost
Shuffles in a labyrinthian somnambulism
Through the convoluted syntax

Of visions lingering amidst the kudzu,
Magnolia, and interwoven vines
That insulate this private place
From Oxford and the world.
Maybe that sinister sound
Is the reverberation of urgent ants

Racing to overtake me before I flee,
Enthrall memory in half-light,
And keep me from making my own reputation
By chaining me to this lawn,
Feeding on meters I plagiarize from silence,
Gnawing the bones of an unknown poet.

Pilgrimage in Harvest Time

A ubiquitous cotton crop
Lines both sides of the road I take
Passing through the Delta
From West Helena to Oxford,
Via Clarksdale, Marks, and Batesville.

Everywhere, biplane dusters
Knot the air into double bow ties;
Their hectic flights remind me of bees
Flitting between blossoms and leaves,
Pollinating white dogwoods.

Frequently I turn sideways
And muse on the profusion of clusters
That blur into a snowy blizzard,
Lose depth, dimension, and perspective;
Blinking brings them back into sync.

This land of compresses, pickers, gins,
And field cages strewn with tufts
Surrounds me like a padded cell
In a desolate sanitarium
Where I've been left to waste away.

I feel crazed, stranded,
Unable to fathom how my nomadic spirit
Ever managed to steer me
So totally astray
From family, home, my noble profession

Of educating children about Milton and Donne.
Suddenly the land to the east expands,
Becomes hills covered in loblolly,
Kudzu, vetch, cedar, and cypress,
Exciting me to the exigencies of my quest.

Just ahead is Rowan Oak.
I hesitate outside its gate,
Afraid, yet impatient, to discover
This new Jerusalem
And sate forever my raging curiosity

To see the place where Faulkner paced,
Meditated, ate, slept,
And wrote with such wit and frantic indignation
That even in death he possesses me.
I kneel, a pilgrim at the Wailing Wall.

As I Lay Sleeping

Although sleep still shoulders my dreams,
Visions of the path salvation takes
Through Bailey's Woods to Rowan Oak
Awaken my restless spirit;
It maneuvers like a biplane crop duster
In Delta planting time,

Deliberately twisting, spiraling,
And soaring over nerves strung taut
Along my spine's poles;
It dives recklessly as a wounded duck,
Recovers just in time
To atomize my blighted psyche with pesticides.

My drowsy body shudders,
Lingers on the brink of consciousness
And sinks back into cerebrations
That might have been plowed, disced, and seeded
By machines guided by "darkies,"
Whose reverberations disturb my breathing.

The soul within my soul recoils
From dust-parched specters of black men
Seated on antique tractors,
Spraying plants by hand from "cain see"
To collied "caint see."
My weevily self-esteem wilts from guilt.

Yet in a matter of steps,
My spirit climbs up out of shadows
Entwined in kudzu and honeysuckle vines,
Arrives at Old Taylor Road,
And, slipping through an opening
In Rowan Oak's magnolia-scented silence,

Surrenders to its seclusion.
Tranquility lifts me above sleep's ashes,
Promising possibilities
For achieving retributive solutions
To abuses unloosed by robed, hooded ghosts
Who, last eve, burned crosses on my dreams.

Bill

For Malcolm Cowley

Only a total madman,
Obsessed with possessing the word-horde,
Deriving through incantation
The identical pleasure
God had known in considering His Creation,
Ever would have presumed to contemplate,
Not to mention execute,
The splendid apostrophes he exploded
Across isolated Yoknapatawpha
From a brain so scintillating
It could shape visions and symbols
From mere sounds, tastes, and scents,
Myths from images as disparate as:

Quentin riding a train, Death's express,
Flushing the same crap
Along tracks
Stretching between his solitary years
In Jefferson, Mississippi,
And iron-cold Boston, and back, just once,
To the stained burl roots
His ancestors dug, shoveled, axed, fired,
At times even Sutpened into latticed
And handcarved gingerbread architecture
Mansioned in magnificent silhouette
Against a trammeled fanlight,
The South . . .

Ike thriving on ancient codes
Revived each season
In an endless Big Woods mythos
Seeded with outsized animals
And people
Neither black, red, white,
Hybrid, old, ancient nor ageless,

* * *

But capable of loving, hating, forgiving,
For whom hunting together
And seeking elusive ghosts alone,
Without defiling the ritual of hot blood
On cold, rainy, autumnal days,
Were the most sacred civil rites of all . . .

Addie traveling in a wagoned coffin
Fastidiously crafted by Cash
To pass through Erebus intact;
Vardaman inside a live fish
Caught and boned by the ambiguities
Of his ten-year-old idiot/genius;
Dewey Dell swelling with unwanted fecundity;
Darl and Jewel saddled to a mad horse,
Clearing the entire sky
In a single nightmare;
And Anse taking a duck-legged wife
As if to repair the rift
In his family's solidarity . . .

These figments of a kindled spirit,
Reaching to speak to spirits
Speaking to each other
In a galaxy resurrected from nonexistence
For the sake of liberating a common soul,
Help explain the perfectly beautiful lunacy
He could never quite contain
Within a solitary sentence
He could never quite refrain from embroidering
With universal gossamer
Into paragraphs he could never quite
Sustain
For the constraints of God's parentheses.

Runners

For Noel Polk and Tom McHaney

Not like high wild geese
Fleeing their back-winging shadows,
But as exhilarated phantoms do we soar
Each morning in liberated cadence
Through the heart's Bailey's Woods
Before the world awakens to our crazy stirrings —
Ghosts of an ancient, insatiable order.

We run as one, we three,
In unassailed camaraderie,
Partaking of the cool, dense-scented solitude
Whose profuse trees admit the shafted sun
Through hidden openings
Like slanted, argentiferous rain.
We run under a mist of heated breath;

Sweat exits our hard-pressed flesh
Like ecstasies emanating from heaven's pores.
Yet there's no oppressiveness
Where the dialectical essence of friendship
Repels fatigue's incursions.
The mesmerical Woods
Anesthetize our pain as we reach into reserves

To rediscover the nature and depth
Of our volition. In luxuriant apotheosis,
Rowan Oak materializes through the cedars
And waxy magnolias. Arrival is sweet cessation.
No matter how transitory,
The moment satisfies the sum of our years.
We admire the silent, Greek edifice

Before turning and reentering the slumberous aura
Whose spongy paths are the labyrinth
We must traverse before day begins.
Deeper and heavier with each step,
Our bodies wade the leafy ocean
That tugs at us, begs us surrender
To its insinuations. We resist, remind ourselves

That finishing is just a matter of distance
While quitting prematurely
Is the denial of pride and fidelity to discipline
We each thrive on and share.
Suddenly daylight discovers us.
Purged and transcendent, we emerge as one,
Bringing word of victory over Xerxes.

Visitation Rites

Each year, the pilgrimage seems to increase.
Those he's touched with mere words
Come to lay praises at his grave,
Contemplate the modesty of his final repose,
And be sanctified or redeemed
By the quietude pervading this pied cemetery.

Annually I make the journey to Oxford alone,
To breathe for a few days
The breeze and humidity,
Listen to the birds' pastoral rhapsodies
That linger in this isolated region
Seventeen years after his death.

It's a humble Grail I quest:
To return to his modest resting place
That I might mingle with his ghost,
Catch fragrant traces of his vagrant presence
Among white oaks standing guard,
And converse with his bones, momentarily,

To reteach myself the nature of austerity
And patience, and be reminded of the privacy
Creation requires. Yet as I sit
On the cement retainer surrounding his plot,
Translating images still white-hot
From God's crucible, an approaching car

Breaks my serene concentration.
I pray it'll leave and that my paean
Will move toward its own conclusion
Without my intellect needing to prod it.
But two women, aiming cameras,
Assail the grave with quizzical speculations,

Not about eschatology but a natal date
Emblazoned in marble — 1897 —
Common to the writer and his wife.
Suddenly, snapping shutters
Riddle the silence like bullets.
Helplessly I watch myself being shot

By a hit-and-miss fusillade
From sophisticated motorized equipment.
No matter how I try to escape
Their rapid-fire desecration, I'm unable.
When I revive, they've disappeared;
But my poetic spirit has died.

Of Books, and Woods, and Us

For Professor James W. Webb

All the fine, signed, limited editions
With decorated gold-stamped bindings,
Uncut rag paper,
And tipped-in colophons
With his minuscule signature affixed

Line my library shelves like potted urns
In catacombs; immolated in stale air,
They wait for worms to eat their glue,
Incandescent lights to fade their spines,
Moisture to fox their pages,

And dryness to break them down to fiber
In the room I no longer use.
Soon even memories of the writing I admired
For transmuting idiots into giants,
Noble Quixotes from slipshod convicts

Will slide into the wide cedar-silence
Of vine-woven senescence
Which slowly embraces my languid mind
In its photosynthetic profusion,
Growing impenetrable

Except to the few who, like Boon,
Will come to the crazytree to meditate
And, breaking their guns in pieces,
Curse the squirrels and snakes
For the world's fantastical mistakes.

Then, in a matter of decades,
The library that confined the books,
Rowan Oak, the home
That guarded his spirit, and Bailey's Woods
Will be, like Campovaccino

Over the Roman Forum,
One vast pasture in which cows and sheep
Graze with implacable unmolestation,
Tended by peaceable shepherds and peasants
Innocent of past and passing days.

The Trysting Place

Seated beneath three white oaks
In the presence of two lesser cedars
Filled with the breeze's suspirations,
My being settles into repose.

Quietude, unintruded by human voices,
Absolves me of earthly ties,
Allows my eyes to follow tracery
Horizontally incised in both stones

Lying side by side at the apex
Of my reverential gaze. One by one,
The chiseled letters multiply,
Change into granite monograms, coalesce,

And, flying into my unfocused vision,
Announce themselves as namesakes,
Two kindred souls rendezvoused by Time
In this timeless trysting place:

Man and lady, writer and wife,
Sepulchered only of bone, hair, and air,
Touch me, share their heritage
Of privacy, modesty, forbearance.

I, in turn, recite my verse for them
As if poetry were the one idiom
Able to translate into all tongues
My heart's need to love someone

Worthy of worship, transcendent.
The combined chorus of our silent voices
Revives the dialogue between God and man
That endows survival with vitality,

Engenders hope of one day discovering
The mystical origins of our kinship.
For now, sleepy William, sweet Estelle,
I leave you. Please wait for me.

Rummaging in the Attic

For my blessed Jan

Bailey's Woods is a Victorian attic
Punctuated by irregularly-placed windows
And crisscrossed with protruding beams
Angling toward cathedraled ceilings
Beneath sweeping eaves and pinnacled roofs;

A magical catchall
Stuffed with fabulous bric-a-brac,
Relics of past decades and generations
Decomposing in various stages of oxidation,
Suffused with dust-mote ghosts,

Buzzing insects, and tiny creatures
Unmolested for seasons
In serenity engendered by few human intrusions.
Only occasional daydreamers
Come to repose, lose themselves for moments

Before descending by ascending
Into the outside universe
Where Time's punctual ukase
Precludes accidental discoveries, reverie, forgetting,
Aery observations, and rarefied insights.

Bailey's Woods is my most secret place
Of escape, my safest retreat
Whenever I have need
To climb the highest peak in my cosmos
And survey the terrain for enemies

Or return to confirm certain memories
Stuffed in nooks, trunks, and on shelves
Are intact. Just yesterday, in fact,
I went upstairs to look for nothing in particular
And found *you* browsing in the shadows.

At Rest

For "Do" Commins
and Franny Commins Bennett

Sweet, sleeping William
Is undistracted by votaries
Kneeling at his grave.

Completely serene
Beneath the grieving earth
Below a white-oak sky,
He's rooted to the other universe
By lines of poetry
God recited
And he translated into prose.

Soon, like descending Moses,
He'll return
With the broken stones — intact.

Genealogists

For Bob Hamblin, friend nonpareil

Once back in my car
Parked just beyond the indefensible gate
Separating Rowan Oak
From Old Taylor Road, Oxford,
And the flocks of cosmic pilgrims
Coming to eavesdrop daily on gods and ghosts,
Gossiping ubiquitously
About William's relinquished domain,
I take off my coat,
Shake the chill from bones
Mid-March has filled with stiffness,
And settle down for the long drive home.

But my senses hold me fast to this place
So isolated and empty and silent
Save for importunate jays,
Docile robins, and sparrows
Whose collective chirping
Is a ceaseless recitation of genealogies
Existing yet in Mississippi's bibles.
My mind listens assiduously to the birds,
Enters their conversations,
And begs to be heard, to be heard
Even as the distance I put between us
Diminishes their voices to whisperousness.

It's my heart, that voluptuous courtesan,
That having spent so many nights
Under the weight of his metaphors
And waking naked on the bed he spread with gardenias,
Desires to remain and confess my presence,
Not my intellect; it's always rejected excess.
I've returned this spring to ask the birds
If his spirit has changed directions
That I might fly in search of him
All the days of my life.
Their answer is his quavering voice
Swelling in the elegiac cedars.

LOUIS DANIEL BRODSKY

Louis Daniel Brodsky was born in St. Louis, Missouri, in 1941, where he attended St. Louis Country Day School. After earning a B.A., Magna Cum Laude, at Yale University in 1963, he received an M.A. in English from Washington University in 1967 and an M.A. in Creative Writing from San Francisco State University the following year.

From 1968 until 1987, while maintaining his writing schedule, he managed a 350-person men's clothing factory and developed a chain of "Slack Outlets" for Biltwell Co., Inc. of St. Louis, Missouri.

Mr. Brodsky is the author of fourteen volumes of poetry. In addition, he has published eight scholarly books on Nobel laureate William Faulkner, and most recently, a biography titled *William Faulkner, Life Glimpses*.

Listing his occupation as Poet, he is also an adjunct instructor at Mineral Area College in Flat River, Missouri, and Curator of the Brodsky Faulkner Collection at Southeast Missouri State University in Cape Girardeau, Missouri.